LEAH'S
SONG

Other Apple paperbacks by
ETH CLIFFORD:

Help! I'm a Prisoner in the Library

Just Tell Me When We're Dead

LEAH'S SONG

ETH CLIFFORD

Original title: The Man Who Sang in the Dark

Illustrated by Mary Beth Owens

AN
APPLE
PAPERBACK

SCHOLASTIC INC.
New York Toronto London Auckland Sydney

ISBN 0-590-42193-X

12 11 10 9 8 7 6 5 4 3 2 1 9/8 0 1 2 3 4/9

Printed in the U.S.A. 28

First Scholastic printing, April 1989

For my grandchildren:
Moshe, Meir, Zahava, Eliahu,
Avraham, Chaim, and Bat-Sheva,
who complete the circle of family love.

LEAH'S SONG

". . . and they lived happily ever after," Leah said as she closed the book she was reading to her four-year-old brother, Daniel.

Daniel's dark-brown eyes were puzzled. "How long is 'ever after'?"

He waited expectantly for his sister's answer. Leah was ten, in fifth grade, and had an answer for everything. Well, almost everything. She could recite the names of all the states alphabetically, do arithmetic in her head without using her fingers, recite poetry, and sharpen pencils with a knife without breaking the point.

Of course Daniel didn't know whether Leah always gave him the *right* answer. Mama said Leah was creative. That meant Leah often made up what she didn't know.

" 'Ever after' means forever and ever," Leah said, then added positively, "and a day."

Daniel shook his head. "People don't live forever and ever. They can't. Can they, Mama?"

Mama bit a thread, snapped it away from the dress she was sewing, and looked up, her eyes sad. "No, Daniel. They can't."

Leah knew Mama was thinking of Papa.

"I didn't say real live people," Leah put in quickly. "Forever and a day is only in stories. In stories, princesses can sleep for a hundred years, and wicked witches can turn princes into frogs. And sorcerers can do magic, like turning lead into gold."

Daniel settled back against his pillow. "Now read me a poem. Not from the book. One that you made up."

Leah not only recited; she acted. Her voice rose and sank. Her hazel eyes narrowed and widened. She used her hands like a dancer, as if each line of her poem ran like a melody through her slender body. Her thick hair, dark as Mama's but cut short in a Dutch boy haircut, bounced as she moved about.

Daniel watched her, entranced. Mama even stopped the whir of the sewing machine to listen.

Each night, as soon as Leah finished, Daniel always begged, "One more, Leah. Please?"

But Mama knew Daniel would ask for another and another. So she said, "Story time is over, Daniel."

No one could argue with Mama when she used that tone.

Leah sighed. The trouble with bedtime for Daniel was that he slept on a cot right here in this room. The one lamp, on the end table opposite his cot, had to be turned off so Daniel could fall asleep. The bedroom, in which Mama and Leah shared a large double bed, had no lamp, only an overhead light. The unshaded bulb hung down from the ceiling. It swung back and forth whenever Mama pulled its long cord to turn it on or off.

Of the two rooms in the apartment, the one in which she read to Daniel was more interesting. It was their kitchen/dining room/living room all in one. A sink, stove, and icebox stood in one corner, along the wall across from the door. Mama's pots and pans hung over the stove, as white as hard scrubbing could make the gleaming enamel surface. A table and three chairs were under the double window that faced the street. Mama had bought them at the secondhand store.

Leah had hated them at first, hated it all — the furniture, these rooms. How quickly everything had changed with Papa gone.

In their other home, the living room (which Papa always called the parlor) was a room all by itself. A heavy couch stood against the long wall. Two pull-up chairs faced the couch on each side. Papa's chair, which was the same soft brown velvet as the couch, was big enough to hold Papa and Leah, and then Daniel, too, all at the same time.

Papa called it the "loving chair," because Leah and Daniel could snuggle in his arms before bedtime and listen to stories he made up each evening, just for them.

Mama, in the smaller matching chair, would glance up from her sewing every once in a while to smile at them and shake her head at Papa's tall tales. Mama was always sewing something, because Papa didn't make enough money in his little tailor shop.

The table and chairs in the dining room had been big and solid, too. Papa wanted furniture that would last. There was even a china closet in which Mama kept dishes and glasses that were used only on special occasions.

The kitchen was sometimes best of all, because when Papa wasn't too tired, he and Leah played games on the smooth dark wood of the kitchen table. When they played checkers, Leah won. When they played dominoes, Leah won.

"Such a smart girl," Papa always marveled. "Who can beat such a clever girl?"

And then, suddenly, Papa was gone. And all the furniture that was meant to last was gone, for Papa had bought it "on time."

Now they were here, and when the secondhand man brought the table and chairs, Leah said, "I hate them. They're ugly."

The secondhand man shrugged his shoulders. He was a heavy man with spiky brown hair and fleshy cheeks that seemed stained a permanent red. He had a habit of winking when he spoke. Leah thought he was making fun of her, but Mama said it was just a nervous habit.

"Ugly is as ugly does," he told Leah, which made no sense to her at all. For good measure, he added, with that knowing wink, "Beggars can't be choosers."

Mama was furious. "We are *not* beggars."

The secondhand man threw up his hands in mock horror. "Excuse me! I should have known. You're Mrs. Rockefeller. And I'm the king of hearts."

Mama paid him in white-lipped anger, while Leah and Daniel stared doubtfully at what Mama claimed was their dining-room set.

When the man left, Mama gave brisk orders. "Daniel, spread the newspapers on the floor. Leah, bring me the paint I left out in the hall. And the brushes. And don't forget the mixing stick."

After Daniel spread the papers, Mama let Leah stir the paint and didn't scold her when some of the paint spilled over onto the newspapers. Then both children watched while Mama painted the chairs and table legs a bright yellow.

The next day, when the paint was thoroughly dry, Mama pasted decals on the broad slats across the top of each chair. Now white daisies with yellow centers danced across the slats.

Later Mama covered the table with a yellow cloth. Around the edge she crocheted a circle of white daisies. Then she placed a bowl of flowers right smack in the middle of the table. The flowers came from the five-and-ten-cent store, but they looked almost real when the sunlight streaming in through the window touched them with gold.

Mama went back to the secondhand store. This time the secondhand man brought a wicker sofa, a wicker arm chair, a small end table, and a lamp.

"Who uses porch furniture in a living room?" he wondered. Then he caught sight of Mama's expression and added hastily, "Listen. I'm only asking, right?"

Mama's face stayed cold. "Now it's porch furniture. When I'm finished, you won't recognize it."

"Hey, lady. If you live long enough, you see miracles," he told Mama, and left.

"He's mean," Daniel said. "I should have kicked him in the leg."

"He would have kicked you back," Leah told him.

Mama laughed. "Never mind. We know what we're doing, don't we?"

Daniel looked at Leah, who nodded.

"Of course we do." She tried to sound like Mama and must have succeeded, because Mama flashed her a loving smile. Mama wasn't a hugging woman, so Leah hugged Daniel instead.

Mama painted all the wicker surfaces white, then covered the worn cushions in what she said were slip-covers. Yellow was Mama's favorite color, and she loved flowers. Soon the sofa and chair matched. Even the sewing machine, next to the end table that held the lamp, had its own cover. Everything in the room glowed.

"Like holding sunshine in your hand," Mama said.

Daniel ran to the window to see if he could cup the sunshine in his hands. But he could not capture the golden light. When he turned, his face was downcast until he saw Mama and Leah laughing. Then his face brightened, and he laughed, too.

Daniel's cot, which Mama got for free from the landlady, Mrs. Safer, was against the wall, facing the wicker sofa. A white candlewick spread turned the narrow cot into a daybed.

"What is a daybed?" Daniel asked.

"A daybed is for sitting on," Mama explained patiently. "At night, it is for sleeping."

When Daniel snuggled down under the covers, Leah sighed again. Now Mama would put out the light, and she and Mama would go into the bedroom. In addition to the double bed, with its white iron headboard, the room had a wide, high dresser, with a picture of Mama and Papa in their wedding clothes.

Next to the window, which faced another street, Mama had placed her rocker. Sometimes Mama sat there, after Leah was asleep, and stared blindly out the window. Leah knew Mama did this, for once in a while when Leah woke briefly, she could see Mama silhouetted against the window, the rocker stilled, and Mama motionless.

"What do you see out there in the dark, Mama?" Leah asked one time.

"The past," Mama replied. "The hopes. The dreams. Don't trouble yourself, Leah. Just go to sleep."

Leah didn't understand Mama's answers, but the sight of Mama in her rocker, a quiet figure against the quiet night sky, was wonderfully comforting.

Mrs. Safer hadn't wanted to rent this two-room apartment on the third floor — the top floor of the building — to Mama, especially when she learned Papa was dead.

"I don't rent to widows with orphans," Mrs. Safer said promptly, that day two weeks ago when Mama, Daniel, and Leah had walked into the grocery store on the ground floor.

The store was in a corner building, so its grimy windows faced two different streets. A sign in each window read ROOMS TO LET. Mama had studied the signs, and peered in through both windows but couldn't see inside. Finally, she took a deep breath and opened the door. A tiny bell tinkled overhead as the door opened. A lady behind the counter looked up. When she saw Mama, Daniel, and Leah, she became wary, but she didn't speak.

Mrs. Safer's gray hair was pulled back into a tight bun at the back of her head. Mama wore her hair the same way, but her hair was a rich, glowing brown, which exactly matched the color of her eyes.

Wispy strands of gray hair escaped from Mrs. Safer's bun, brushing across the nape of her neck and flying up around her ears. She flicked them away impatiently from time to time. Mama's hair was orderly, held firmly in place with long thick hairpins.

Mrs. Safer's eyes were a tired, weak gray under scraggly gray eyebrows. Her face was heavily lined, and Leah wondered if she had forgotten how to smile.

Mama's face was still smooth, even though she was quite old. Leah knew Mama was almost thirty-five. And she had no wrinkles at all, unless one counted the small ones around her mouth and eyes.

In case Mama hadn't heard her, Mrs. Safer repeated in a louder voice, "I don't rent to widows with orphans."

Leah looked down at the floor so she wouldn't see the hurt in Mama's eyes. Now that Papa was gone, Mama couldn't pay the rent on their old apartment. But everywhere she went, landlords turned her away. No one wanted to rent rooms to a widow.

Mama held her head higher, pushed her shoulders back. She was a small woman, but she carried herself tall. "My children are not orphans. They have me."

"Wonderful!" Mrs. Safer snapped back. Leah wondered why she was so angry. "They have you," Mrs. Safer went on. "Now, when people are thrown out of work right and left, when grown men are selling apples on the streets to make a living, you tell me your children have you. And who do *you* have? Who will pay *your* rent, Mrs. Widow Lady?"

Mama's eyes blazed. "I will pay it. On the dot. I am clever with a needle. Already I have some good customers."

A man had come from behind the store, a short, lean, meek-looking man, with a large apron tied round his middle. As he listened to the women, his pale blue eyes grew sad.

Mama turned to him quickly. "Are you Mr. Safer? Maybe I can talk to you . . ."

Mr. Safer cut Mama off. "I heard." He turned to his wife. "Rent her the rooms."

"*She* will pay seven dollars a month?"

Mrs. Safer didn't notice how Mama bit her lips when she heard how much money she would have to pay.

"If she can't pay, she'll owe. She won't be the first to owe us money."

Mama assured Mr. Safer, "You won't be sorry. I promise."

"Listen, these are hard times for everybody," Mr. Safer replied. "So if we are not for one another, who will be?"

The hard times had a name — the Depression. The whole country suffered from it. Mama had explained it to Leah, who now, in turn, explained it to Mrs. Safer, in case she didn't understand.

"It's the Depression." Leah made the word important, *Depression* with a capital *D*, the way Mama and the other grownups did.

"So! She is not only pretty. She is smart, too," Mr. Safer marveled.

He reached into a large glass container on the counter and pulled out two crystal-clear formless shapes, with strings running through them. "Here. One for you. And one for the little person. Rock candy."

Daniel stuffed his piece into his mouth at once, like a squirrel storing acorns in its pouch.

Leah put her piece in her pocket, for later. That way she would enjoy it twice, once in the getting and again, later on, in the eating.

Mrs. Safer continued to eye Leah and Daniel with suspicion. "Such small children. They will run up and down the steps all day long. They will play ball in the hall. I can just imagine how they will jump on the stairs. It will be noisy."

"No. My children know how to behave. They will be quiet," Mama said.

Mr. Safer turned, reached behind the counter, and removed a key from a large hook.

"Listen, Mrs. . . . Mrs. . . . ?"

"Berk."

"Mrs. Berk. Here is the key to your apartment. Good luck and God bless you," he said.

Unexpectedly, Mama's eyes filled with tears. Leah knew why. At last they were not being turned away.

"You won't regret this," Mama whispered. "I thank you. For myself and my children, I thank you."

Mr. Safer waved away her thanks. "What am I giving you? The keys to the kingdom? Stay, and be welcome. Right, Hilda?" he asked his wife.

Mrs. Safer nodded. She leaned closer to Mama. "Believe me, Mrs. Berk. I am not such a hard woman as I sound. But we are getting older. I worry. I see the money going out, and not coming in. People need groceries, can we say no? But we have to live also . . ."

Mama reached across the counter to take Mrs. Safer's hand in her own.

"I understand, Mrs. Safer. Trust me. That's all I ask. Please trust me."

Mr. Safer blew his nose hard. "Enough talking," he commanded. "Go. Look at the rooms."

Mama closed her hand around the key, then followed Mrs. Safer through the store into a large kitchen.

At the far side of the room, a door led into a narrow hall. Mrs. Safer pointed to another door.

"This is your entrance to the hall, not through the store," she explained.

Leah opened the door and peeked out.

"Mama, it leads right out into the street."

"I want to see, too," Daniel said.

"He always has to do everything I do," Leah complained, but she held the door open for him just the same.

Mrs. Safer began climbing the steps, slowly, her hand clutching the banister. Mama and Leah and Daniel followed.

"It's dark in this place," Daniel said. He grabbed Leah's hand. "I can't see."

Mrs. Safer grumbled, "What's to see? Steps. And more steps. For this you need to see?"

Mama frowned at Daniel and put her fingers to her lips. But Leah understood how Daniel felt. It *was* dark. That was bad enough. But at the end of each half-flight of steps was a landing, and on each landing a small bulb sent out feeble green light, strange, eery light. In that dim light, shadows leaped ahead, beside, and behind them.

"I'm never going to come up and down these steps by myself," Leah swore to herself. "Never."

On the third floor, Mrs. Safer walked the length of a long narrow hallway. At the end, she opened a door. Leah and Daniel rushed in, but Mama stood at the door, as if reluctant to enter.

Mrs. Safer patted Mama's shoulder and left.

Daniel came running back to Mama.

"Are you sad, Mama?" he asked, anxiously.

Mama walked into the room, looked around, went into the second room, and studied that, too. Then she answered Daniel.

"Sad? Of course not. Wait till you see what we'll do with these rooms. A visit to the secondhand store, some cans of paint . . . in a little while you won't recognize this place. It will be like a palace."

Leah smiled. "Good, Mama. I've always wanted to live in a palace."

"Me, too," Daniel echoed.

Leah and Mama looked at each other, their eyes dancing.

Just then there was a faint knock on the door. Leah ran to open it. Mrs. Safer was rushing away as fast as her tired old legs could take her. On the floor, next to the open door, was a basket of groceries, including a quart of milk and a dozen eggs.

"Mama! Look!"

Mama picked up the basket, then put her hand to

her lips. Leah could tell Mama was deeply moved.

"You see, children?" Mama said, when she could speak. "We have made a wonderful new beginning. We have come home."

CHAPTER 3

In the two weeks they had lived in their new home, Leah had gone up and down the steps many times, always reluctantly. Sometimes Mama sent her down to the grocery to buy food. This evening Mama needed eggs. "Leah. Ask Mrs. Safer for a dozen brown eggs," Mama instructed. "Be sure to give her this dime."

Leah gave Mama a woeful glance. "Do I have to go?"

"Yes. You have to. Now."

"Suppose there's somebody waiting on the steps!" Leah's voice quavered.

"Nobody waits," Mama told Leah firmly. "Don't let your imagination run away with you."

But Mama didn't understand. *Shadows* waited — quiet, deathly quiet, shadows. They lingered on the landings; they leaped up the walls, lengthening in front of her, shortening beside her, looming up behind her.

During the day, light filtered in through a skylight in the ceiling over the third floor landing. But the moment the daylight faded, the shadows gathered again. And they waited. Leah could *feel* them waiting.

Now, with dragging feet, Leah made her way down the long hallway. When she reached the flight of steps going down, she took a deep breath, and glanced back at the lamplight that streamed into the hall behind her, where Daniel was safe with Mama.

She scolded herself. Wasn't she ten years old? She wasn't a little kid like Daniel. She should be brave. That's what Mama had told them after Papa died.

"We must all be brave."

But they hadn't lived on the third floor of an old building then.

She thrust her shoulders back and put a foot forward, as if she were testing deep water. She began the downward journey, tiptoeing step by step. That way no one would hear a frightened ten-year-old girl coming down.

When she almost reached the second-floor landing, she sagged against the banister with relief. Why, she was halfway down and nothing had happened.

Mama was right. Her imagination was too active.

Leah moved with more confidence now. Just a few more steps, and she would be on the landing. At that moment, she heard a tapping sound. Her foot froze in midair.

Someone — some *thing* — was coming up to meet her.

She turned to flee back upstairs, but paused. Perhaps it would be better to race past it, whatever it was, to the safety of Mrs. Safer's kitchen.

The tapping sound came nearer.

Leah leaned over the railing, careful to keep out of sight. She saw the shadow first. It was so high on the wall that it turned and stretched across part of the ceiling.

Her glance moved down to the figure on the steps that created the looming shadow.

A tall, thin man, one hand clutching the banister, one hand holding a cane, was inching his way upstairs.

Sneaking upstairs, Leah thought.

He was dressed all in black — a black hat that hid his face, a long black coat. Even his cane was black.

It was the cane that made the tapping sound. From under the hat, from the lips Leah couldn't see, came a low humming.

Suddenly there flashed into Leah's mind the memory of a bird that once had become trapped in her

classroom. Wildly, it flew round and round the room. Its tiny heart fluttered so hard Leah imagined for a moment she could see the movement. It beat its wings against the window, until Leah had leaped from her seat to open the window and free the bird.

She was that bird now, her heart fluttering. Leah had no wings, but she could surely fly up the steps.

Suddenly the man spoke. "Is someone there?"

Leah gasped. How had he seen her from under his hat?

The man rapped his cane angrily on the step. "Who's there? Speak up. What do you want?"

"It's only me," Leah whispered. Tears welled in her eyes, trembled on her cheeks.

"Who is 'me'? I insist you speak up."

"It's me. Leah. From the third floor. We just moved here two weeks ago."

The man seemed to go limp. He leaned against the banister. When he spoke again, his voice was filled with anger. "You frightened me half to death."

Leah stared at him in surprise. A grown-up, afraid? How was that possible? She had never seen Mama afraid.

"Are you making fun of me?" Leah demanded. "I'm only ten years old. How could I scare you? I'm only a kid." Then she remembered her own terror and accused him. "You scared me on purpose, didn't you?"

"Oh you poor child," the man said at once. "I'm so sorry. I'm a new tenant. I have a room on the second floor."

Leah said with resentment, "Why were you sneaking up the steps? Didn't you see me? Didn't you know you were scaring a little kid?"

The man dropped his head. Then, slowly, he lifted it, and removed his hat. He stared up at her with unblinking eyes.

"No, child," he told her. "I didn't see you. I'm blind."

CHAPTER 4

"*Blind*?"

Leah shrank back against the wall. Why did that one word make the shadows move closer, the dim green light spookier?

She glanced upstairs. She wanted to go back to Mama and safety, but the dime she clutched in her hand reminded her that Mama expected her to buy a dozen brown eggs.

The blind man coughed. Startled, Leah gasped, and dropped the coin. It fell step to step, spun briefly, then stopped on the landing just below.

"Leah." The man's voice was gentle. "Please. Don't be afraid."

When Leah didn't respond, he continued in a reasonable tone, "After all, you can run. You know for sure I can't run after you. Can I? Can I?" he repeated insistently.

She moved away from the wall, to peer down over the banister. Even though he had removed his hat, she couldn't see him clearly, for he was still a shadow lost in shadows.

"You couldn't chase me. I'm a very fast runner."

"See? Then you know you are safe. Now then, did I hear a coin drop?"

"A dime. I have to buy eggs for Mama."

"So. Let us see how we can solve our problem. You are on the steps just above the landing?"

Leah nodded, then remembered he couldn't see her. "Yes."

"And I am just below the landing. Listen to me, Leah. I am going to come up the steps. When I reach the landing, I will turn *away* from you and walk down the hall to my room. You can watch me every minute. When I am out of the way, you can come down and run your errand. I promise not to be on the steps or in the hall when you come back. Agreed?"

When she didn't respond, he said in a gentle voice. "You must speak, child. I can't see a nod."

"Agreed," Leah said.

She watched warily as he extended his cane, moved up one slow step at a time, one hand feeling its way upward on the banister. At the landing, he turned and placed his left hand on the wall, tapping his cane firmly against the wood floor with his right hand.

Leah tiptoed down to the landing, making certain that he opened his door and closed it behind him. Only then did she pick up the dime and race downstairs.

Her errand done, Leah flew back up the steps. Heart pounding, she burst into the third-floor apartment.

"Mama!" Daniel cried out in alarm. "Something's the matter with Leah."

Mama turned away from the stove to stare. "What is it? What's happened?"

"A blind man. There was a blind man on the steps," Leah sobbed.

Mama's hand flew to her heart. "Did he hurt you? *What did he do?*"

"He scared me, that's what he did. Mama, he's *blind!*"

"Don't ever frighten me like that again." Mama was so relieved, she was furious. "I thought . . . never mind what I thought. Go and wash your face with cold water. Then come help me set the table."

Mama's cold voice upset Daniel. He went close to Leah and took her hand. "You want me to come to the bathroom with you?"

Leah smiled at his protective air. "I'm all right, Daniel. I'm always all right when I'm with you and Mama."

After supper, Leah helped Mama clear the table, then sat down to do her homework. Daniel sat down opposite her.

"I have homework, too." He scribbled lines across the page, mimicking Leah.

Mama went to her sewing machine. The steady whir as she sewed made Leah feel safe, secure.

And then there came a knock on the door.

"I'll get it! I'll get it!" Daniel raced to the door. It might be Mr. Safer, who every once in a while brought Daniel and Leah some little treat from the store.

At the sight of a stranger in the doorway, Daniel drew back. Mama was up and beside him instantly.

"Yes? Can I help you?"

At the frostiness of her voice, the man frowned. "Please," he said. "Are you the little girl's mother?"

"Yes."

"I came up to apologize. And to explain. I didn't know the child was on the steps. Evidently I terrified her. I understand." He pointed to his eyes. "It came as a shock to her. I'm Mrs. Safer's nephew. My name is Gideon Brown. I've just moved in on the second floor. Is she all right?"

Mama stepped back. "Come in, Mr. Brown. I am Mrs. Berk. Leah is fine. She sometimes lets her imagination run wild. I'm sorry if she hurt your feelings."

Gideon Brown took a few steps forward, then paused. Leah stared at him from the safety of the table across the room. How different he looked in the light of the lamp.

The black hat and coat were gone. His hair was gold; it curled tightly around his head, flowed down the sides of his face into a mustache, and ended in a short pointed beard. His eyebrows joined in one thick line across his broad forehead. His nose was large and straight.

He reminded Leah of the picture of a Viking seafarer in her history book. He even had the bright blue eyes of the Viking. But this man's eyes were blank, as if all light had died behind them.

Gideon Brown was as tall as the seafarer, too. Standing beside Mama, he made her seem much smaller than she was.

Mama said, "Since you are a neighbor, and we will be meeting from time to time on the steps, I would like my children to get used to you." She hesitated, then went on, "I hope you understand what I'm saying."

"I understand very well. Even adults find it uncomfortable around me."

"Yes," Mama agreed.

"At least you are honest," Gideon Brown told her.

"You've already met Leah."

"Dramatically," Mr. Brown said.

He had heard the smile in Mama's voice, Leah thought, because he turned to smile back at Mama.

"And this boy standing beside me is Daniel, who is four. Say hello to Mr. Brown, Daniel," Mama prompted him.

Daniel shook his head stubbornly. "I can't."

Mama was puzzled. "You can't? Why not?"

"Because he's blind."

Mama was embarrassed. "Daniel! What a mean thing to say."

"No, no, Mrs. Berk. Not mean. Just honest. Don't scold him. I thought it funny." Gideon Brown threw back his head and laughed. Unexpectedly, Mama joined him.

Leah was surprised. She hadn't heard Mama laugh in a long time, not since Papa died.

Daniel glanced from one to the other.

"I made a joke, didn't I?" he said with delight. "It was funny, wasn't it?"

"Yes, Daniel. It certainly was," Gideon Brown told him.

Again Mama urged him to come in, and again he refused.

"No, no. I didn't come to visit. I wanted to check on Leah. And I also wanted to explain that I am a musician. That's how I make my living. You will probably hear me playing the guitar and singing when I am in my room. If it disturbs you, I want you to let me know."

"Music never disturbs us, Mr. Brown."

"Then I will say good night to you. Good night, Daniel. Good night, Leah."

Leah didn't respond. She had not yet forgiven him for scaring her. And the open sightless eyes made her uneasy.

It was not until Daniel was asleep on the cot and Leah lying on her side of the big double bed, that music drifted upward from the blind man's room.

Mama was in her rocker. When she heard the music, she stopped staring out the window. Instead, she closed her eyes, leaned back in the rocker, and listened.

Leah stared at the ceiling and dreamed. Were there beautiful words to the music? All she could hear were the sweet flowing sounds the blind man plucked from his guitar. There must be words, for she could hear his deep voice but not what he sang. She began to write lines of poetry in her mind.

I can dance like an elf
On the petals of a rose.

Were elves that tiny? Well, why not? Now she would have to think of a rhyming line to go with rose. Doze? Froze? Clothes!

She giggled softly at the thought that had just popped into her head. She recited her new poem in a whisper, just to hear how it sounded. After all, poetry was meant to be heard.

I can dance like an elf

On the petals of a rose.
Or can laugh all by myself
When I wear my laughing clothes.

What a funny nice idea. Wouldn't it be wonderful if Mama could make laughing clothes?

She would ask Mama first thing in the morning.

She sighed, and didn't know she sighed.

Her eyes closed. She slept, and dreamed on.

CHAPTER 5

And so several days passed by. Each night, as music wafted upward, Leah added a few more lines to her poem.

Then, one day when Leah came home from school, she found Daniel waiting for her at the third floor landing. When he heard her footsteps, he shouted down over the banister, "Leah! Guess what! We're going to a party. A tea party."

Leah stopped to stare up at Daniel. Then she bounded up the stairs. A tea party! How extraordinary.

"Mrs. Safer is giving the party." Daniel bubbled over with information. "In her kitchen. After supper. And she'll have cake and something extra for *us*. That's what she said. Something extra."

Leah raced past Daniel, who yelled, "Wait for me! Wait for me!"

He was at her heels when she burst into the room where Mama sat and sewed.

"Yes," Mama said, at the sight of Leah's excited expression. "Right after supper we're going downstairs to Mrs. Safer's."

"What's the something special, Mama?"

Mama shook her head. "If we knew, it wouldn't be a surprise, would it?"

Daniel had a wonderful idea. "Let's eat supper now. Then we can go to the party right away."

"At three o'clock in the afternoon? No, Daniel. First Leah must do her homework."

"Do it. Do it." Daniel pushed Leah toward the table. When she sat down, opened her books, and at last picked up her pencil, he watched anxiously as she began to form her letters. Her teacher, Miss Bankston, had praised Leah's handwriting. Now Leah took special care with all her assignments.

Daniel nudged her. "Can't you write faster?"

Mama rose from the sewing machine and quickly dumped clothespins on Daniel's cot. "Oh, dear," Mama told Daniel. "Look at this. I'll never get all these clothespins back in the bag."

"I can do that." Daniel seated himself on the cot and

began to throw the clothespins into the net bag. Some he threw in one at a time. Others he clamped together. Then he stuck two clothespins together at an angle. "I'm a cowboy," he announced. He grabbed the broom from its place beside the icebox. "This is my horse."

Daniel galloped around the room on the broom, waving his gun and shouting, "Giddyap! Giddyap!"

Leah looked up from her homework with a frown. "You're making too much noise. Can't you be a quiet horse?"

Mama nodded agreement. "Remember my promise to Mrs. Safer," she reminded him.

"But I don't have anything to do," he complained. "Isn't it *ever* going to be time to eat?"

Leah made a paper airplane which Daniel flew busily until Mama finally announced that just this once they would eat early.

At supper time, Daniel began to gulp his food. Mama told him sternly, "If you don't eat properly, no tea party."

Daniel sighed and looked up at the clock. Leah grinned. Daniel couldn't tell time. Still, she knew exactly how he felt.

At long last, it was time to go downstairs. Mama put two bows in Leah's hair, one on each side. She examined Daniel's hands and face and even the area behind his ears. Then they were ready.

Mr. Safer opened the door when Mama knocked. "Well, look who's here! Come in. Come in."

Daniel started to rush in, then retreated and clung to Mama.

The blind man was in the kitchen, seated in a chair at the far side of the table.

Leah hesitated in the doorway. How could anyone have a tea party with a blind man?

Mama moved Daniel and Leah firmly into the kitchen. There Mr. Safer placed Mama next to Gideon Brown, Leah next to Mama, and Daniel between himself and Mrs. Safer.

"Now." Mr. Safer rubbed his hands together. "All the honored guests are here. The party commences."

Mrs. Safer placed a large chocolate cake in the center of the table. Some of the chocolate icing had dribbled down onto the plate.

"Is that it? Is that the something special?" Daniel sounded disappointed, even though he loved chocolate cake. But that was what Mama baked once in a while.

Mrs. Safer shook her head. "It's coming. Just a few more minutes."

But first Mrs. Safer placed a glass in front of each

adult. Leah knew why. Tea tasted better in a glass, Mama had told her. Then Mrs. Safer put a glass bowl filled with small sugar cubes on the table, too. Mr. Safer promptly popped a cube between his teeth and sipped his tea through the cube. Mama dropped two cubes into her glass and stirred them gently.

"Is it almost time for the special?" Daniel asked, anxious lest Mrs. Safer had forgotten.

"The time is now." Mrs. Safer went to the stove. When she returned to the table, she set a cup in front of Daniel and one in front Leah.

"What is it?" Leah asked.

"Hot chocolate. With real whipped cream on top."

Sometimes, as a treat, Mama made cocoa, which she mixed with water and sugar and just a touch of milk. But Leah and Daniel had never even heard of hot chocolate — or seen real whipped cream.

Daniel used his spoon to swirl the whipped cream into the hot chocolate, delighting in the way it foamed in the drink. Then he gulped it down, almost emptying the cup in one swallow. Leah dipped her spoon delicately into the whipped cream, then let it melt on her tongue, savoring this new taste. Then she sipped the hot chocolate. It was incredibly smooth and rich and delicious.

If I live to be a hundred, Leah told herself, I will never forget this drink.

After the dishes were cleared from the table, Mrs. Safer announced, "And now Gideon will sing for us."

Mama leaned back the way she did at night in her rocker and waited, with closed eyes, to hear the music the blind man sang in the dark of his room. But her eyes flew open when he said, "No sad songs tonight. For a party, there must only be happy songs, funny songs."

The first was about "Great Granddad," who lived out West when the West was young. Great Granddad was a busy man who cooked his grub in a frying pan. He picked his teeth with a hunting knife, and wore the same suit all his life.

Mama sat up straight and smiled. Mr. Safer clapped his hands in time to the music. Even Mrs. Safer, who had looked almost half-asleep a moment before, came wide awake, her eyes bright and twinkling with good humor.

The next song was about a young man who took his girl to a restaurant. She said she wasn't hungry, but, Gideon sang, "this is what she ate: a dozen raw, a plate of slaw, a chicken and a roast; some applesass, and sparagrass, and soft-shell crabs on toast; a big box stew,

and crackers, too. Her appetite was immense! When she called for pie, I thought I'd die, for I only had fifty cents!"

Mama smiled again, the same kind of smile she used to give Papa when he told his tall tales.

Leah looked around; how good it was, to be here, now, in this time and this place, she thought.

Daniel seemed spellbound, staring open-mouthed at Gideon Brown. Leah knew how her brother felt. She, too, had watched in wonder at the sure way Gideon Brown's fingers moved across his instrument; had wondered, too, how a blind man could sing such happy tunes.

While Gideon Brown played, Daniel moved closer.

"How do you see to do that?" he asked, when Gideon Brown stopped playing.

"I see with my fingers, Daniel."

"No, you don't. You have to see with your eyes," Daniel objected.

"I can see your face with my fingers, if you'll let me."

"Will it hurt?"

The blind man laughed. "No. I promise."

Daniel held up his face. The blind man's fingers moved with a feather touch around Daniel's forehead, down his nose, across his lips and his chin.

"What a handsome boy you are, Daniel," he said, after a moment.

"Can I see you now?" Daniel asked.

The blind man didn't laugh, just held still, as Daniel, his eyes wide and serious, felt Mr. Brown's face.

Leah watched them with envy. Why couldn't she be like Daniel? But the thought of being that close to the blind man, the blue eyes blank and unseeing, still sent a chill up her spine. And yet his music drew her. Maybe someday she would overcome her fear . . .

Mama rose from the table, a signal that the evening was over. When Daniel protested, Mama sent him a warning glance.

"Wait," the blind man said. "I have one more song just for Daniel and Leah." He smiled. "This one you will surely like."

And like it they did, for they both loved the words and the music set their feet tapping.

When it was over, Mama shook Mr. Brown's hand, holding it firmly in her own. She motioned to Leah to do the same.

Almost as if he could see Mama's gesture, the blind man said, "No, not yet. Leah will shake my hand when we are friends."

Mama's voice was warm and friendly. "Thank you for the music. It has brought joy to all of us."

As Mama and Daniel and Leah went up the steps, Daniel sighed. "It's the best tea party I've ever been to. Wasn't it, Leah?"

She didn't answer. Instead, dancing up the steps, she began to sing the last tune Mr. Brown had played.

There's a little white duck
Sitting in the water,
Little white duck,
Doing what she ought-er.
She took a bite of a lily pad
Flapped her wings and said, "I'm glad
I'm a little white duck
Sitting in the water.
Quack, quack, quack."

She even remembered all the words about the green frog, and the black bug, and the red snake.

Leah sang them up all the steps, from landing to landing, the dark forgotten, safe with Mama and Daniel. She sang them down the long hall, and only stopped short at the sight of a woman leaning against their door.

"It's Mrs. Alpert," Daniel shouted, and ran happily toward the woman. "You know what? We just went to a tea party. The blind man sang lots of funny songs, and he looked at me with his fingers. . . ."

"Come in. Come in," Mama unlocked the door. "Have you been waiting long?"

Leah looked at Mama with surprise. She knew this was an unexpected visit, but Mama didn't show it in her voice or her manner.

"I'll make us some tea," Mama went on.

"Please. Don't bother," Mrs. Alpert said, but Mama was already busy in the kitchen.

Mrs. Alpert sat on the cot with Daniel. She was taller than Mama. She had beautiful hands, Leah thought, so long and graceful, the nails polished, a

ring sparkling on her finger. Her fair hair caught the light of the lamp as she leaned over Daniel; her large light-brown eyes were soft with love as she listened to him.

Mama often said it was a shame Mrs. Alpert had no children, for she was a woman with love to spare.

Mrs. Alpert was one of Mama's best customers, even though she lived in West Philadelphia, which was quite a distance from the South Philadelphia neighborhood Mama and Leah and Daniel called home.

Leah sometimes thought that Mrs. Alpert gave

Mama extra work so she could visit Mama during the day just to see Daniel. She often took Daniel to the school playground, or treated him to an ice cream cone, or took him back to her house for the day.

Mama was grateful, for it gave her time to work without interruption and deliver the clothing she made without having to worry about Daniel.

But Mrs. Alpert had never come in the evening before. Leah could tell Mama was worried at this unexpected visit, though she served the tea to Mrs. Alpert, who sipped it dutifully, and Mama pretended to drink tea, too. Still Mrs. Alpert didn't speak. So after a while Mama asked, her eyes anxious though she kept her voice steady, "Is there a problem about taking Daniel for tomorrow?"

Mama had a big job next day. She had designed a wedding gown for the daughter of one of her customers, a lady named Leffel. Harriet Leffel, the bride-to-be, kept changing her mind about the gown. Finally it was decided that Mama must spend the day at the Leffels' until the gown was finished.

"But no children," Mrs. Leffel had warned. "We're too nervous to have small children under foot at a time like this."

"Leah will be in school, but I cannot leave Daniel," Mama began.

Mrs. Alpert, who was visiting the Leffels, promptly offered to take Daniel for the day, and Leah as well, if Mama wanted Leah to stay home from school.

Leah objected. Miss Bankston had promised to read one of Leah's poems aloud to the class. And so it was settled. Except that Mrs. Alpert was here now, instead of tomorrow morning.

"No, no," Mrs. Alpert reassured Mama. "No trouble. It's just that tomorrow our Women's Club has planned a picnic in the park, with pony rides for the young children, and a clown to entertain them. We want to start early, so I thought, if you didn't mind, that I could take Daniel home with me tonight."

"Tonight?" Mama looked stunned. "But Daniel has never been away from me at night before."

Mrs. Alpert laughed. "But Daniel is such a big boy now. It will be an adventure for him. And Daniel and I always have fun together, don't we, Daniel?"

Daniel nodded, but he seemed a little doubtful. "You want me to sleep in your house the whole night?"

Leah felt a stab of alarm. Daniel was so little. And Mrs. Alpert didn't have children. How would she know what to do if Daniel woke up out of a nightmare, as he sometimes did? Suppose he had to go to the bathroom and was too embarrassed to ask Mrs. Alpert to put the light on for him?

Besides, Daniel couldn't go to sleep unless Leah read a story to him. And then recited a poem, especially her own.

"You'll have to come back tomorrow," Leah said. "Daniel needs me."

Daniel nodded. "Leah has to tell me a story . . ."

Mrs. Alpert laughed. "I will read you as many stories as you like. And I will make you a cup of hot chocolate before you go to sleep . . ."

". . . with whipped cream?" Daniel asked greedily.

"With whipped cream. Or with a marshmallow. What do you say, Daniel?"

Daniel beamed his approval. As soon as Mama got Daniel ready for an overnight visit, he put his hand trustingly into Mrs. Alpert's, dropped it to give Mama and Leah one last hug and kiss, and seized Mrs. Alpert's hand once more. Mama and Leah could hear his voice as he and Mrs. Alpert went down the hall; it trailed back to them as he went down the steps.

How quiet the room was, suddenly. How strange Daniel's bed looked, with Daniel missing from it.

Leah felt angry with Mama, and with Daniel. But most of all, she was upset with Mrs. Alpert.

"She had no right to take Daniel. No right at all. That was a mean thing to do."

Mama sighed. "Mrs. Alpert is only trying to help

us, Leah. Think back. Do you remember what it was like, the first time we met her?"

Leah nodded. She remembered it clearly.

The first time they saw Mrs. Alpert was after Papa died. There was no money, and Mama couldn't find work. One morning she said, "Leah. Daniel. How would you like to go on a long trolley ride?"

"How long?" Daniel demanded instantly. Sometimes he felt sick on a trolley; at least, both times he had traveled on one, his stomach tried to climb right up into his throat.

"We'll have to change trolleys," Mama admitted. "It will be quite a while."

Leah was delighted; it sounded like an adventure, but Daniel looked unhappy until Mama promised he could suck on peppermint candy all the way.

Leah and Daniel were fascinated by the changing

neighborhoods through which they passed. At first there were crowded streets exactly like the one where they lived; then business areas, with stores and offices and large buildings into which people rushed while other people rushed out; finally, there were streets with trees — wide, pleasant streets.

And after what Daniel said accusingly was "forever," they left the second trolley and began to walk.

Daniel was wide-eyed, his mouth open as he looked all around. Leah knew just how he felt.

Did real people live in places like these? In this wonderland, clipped green lawns led to beautiful houses. Large trees shaded the walks; flowering bushes made the air fragrant.

"Are we still in America?" Daniel asked.

"That's dumb," Leah said. "Of course we are."

Mama smiled down at Daniel as she explained, "We're not only still in America. We're still in the same city. This part of the city is called West Philadelphia."

Now Mama gave them both strict instructions. "I am going to walk up to each house. I want you both to wait on the sidewalk each time and be very quiet, understand?"

So Leah and Daniel silently watched as Mama went to each house in turn, to ask for work as a seamstress, or dressmaker. Sometimes, when she rang a bell, a door would open and close at once. A few doors stayed firmly shut. But Mama wouldn't give up. She kept on going up and down the street. At the last house, a woman spoke to Mama, glanced at Leah and Daniel, and beckoned to them.

The woman was Mrs. Alpert, who invited them all in with a welcoming smile.

"I was about to have lunch," she told Mama. "Just

a snack, really. Please join me. It's no fun to eat alone."

They followed her to the back of the house, into a large, cheerful room with a window wall that faced the back garden. Next to the window wall was a round table with six padded chairs.

Leah saw the look in Mama's eyes as she studied the garden. She slipped her hand into Mama's, and they stood together, drinking in the beauty of this back yard.

Mrs. Alpert served thick hot soup in bowls with double handles. The rolls were hot from the oven and dripped with butter. She made tea for Mama and herself. Though she didn't seem to be watching, she gave them all second helpings as soon as their soup was gone, even though Mama protested.

Leah couldn't help thinking that at home she and Daniel never had second helpings of anything, and that Mama always ate sparingly. Apples and other fruit were cut in half and shared by Leah and Daniel. If Mama treated them to a two-cent ice-cream cone, Leah and Daniel took turns licking it.

Now, while they ate, Mama explained her need for work. Her voice was stiff. She was begging; Leah knew it, and she knew, too, how bad it made Mama feel, for Mama was a proud woman.

"Just give me material and I will make a dress for you without charge, so you can see if you like my work."

"No," said Mrs. Alpert.

Mama's face changed. She rose, then sat down again when Mrs. Alpert said, "Never offer to work for free. Make a dress for me and I will pay, like it or not. If I *do* like the dress, I will find other customers for you among my friends."

Leah could see tears glisten in Mama's eyes. She struggled to speak, but couldn't.

Quickly, Mrs. Alpert began to ask Daniel questions. She even took Leah and Daniel into the back yard.

Leah gazed at Mrs. Alpert thoughtfully. She could tell that Mrs. Alpert wanted to give Mama time to cry a little, to let her tears of joy and relief flow freely without anyone watching.

"You're a nice lady," Daniel said.

"And you're the nicest boy I have ever met," Mrs. Alpert told him, beaming. "A wonderful boy."

Leah noticed that every once in a while, as if she couldn't help it, Mrs. Alpert stroked Daniel's hair, or touched his nose gently with a teasing finger, or squeezed his hand in hers.

When they returned, Mama said, "We must leave

now. But I'll come back tomorrow for the material you are going to buy."

"Bring Daniel," Mrs. Alpert said, smiling down at him.

And Mrs. Alpert kept her word. She did get customers for Mama. And Mama was grateful. She always said, "I owe Mrs. Alpert so much. I hope someday I can repay her for her goodness."

Mama broke into Leah's thoughts.

"Now that you've remembered, do you feel better about Daniel spending the night with Mrs. Alpert?"

"Is that the way you're thanking her, Mama?"

"It's such a small favor," Mama said. "And Daniel will be here when you come home from school tomorrow."

"But I feel so lonely."

"Come," Mama said. "Sit here, next to me. And for a change, I will read to you."

"*Alice in Wonderland.*" Leah smiled at last, and snuggled in close to Mama as she began to read.

After a while, Mama looked at the clock and said, "School tomorrow. It's bedtime."

But when Leah was ready for bed, Mama took Leah to the rocker, and held her the way Papa used to in his "loving chair." And as they rocked, Mama sang, "Sleep, my child, and peace attend thee, all through the night."

And Leah was content. Though the family circle had been broken, even if only for one night, Mama's gentle voice gathered her in and comforted Leah.

CHAPTER 8

Daniel bubbled over with details about his stay when Mrs. Alpert brought him home the next day. She was hardly out the door when Daniel reported, "You know what? I had a room all to myself, with circus pictures all over the walls, and an elephant lamp, and a real bed." He made a face at the cot. "And Mother Claire gave me a big clown doll to sleep with . . ."

Mama's head swiveled sharply. "*Mother Claire?*"

"So I wouldn't feel strange and lonesome. And Father Doc gave me a ride on his back . . ."

Leah's brows furrowed a deep frown between her eyes. "Father *Doc?*"

"Mrs. Alpert's husband is a doctor," Mama explained. Her face was a storm cloud.

Daniel didn't notice, just chattered on. Mama is

upset, too, Leah told herself. They hadn't expected Daniel to have such a good time. Leah shook her head in confusion. Why shouldn't it have been fun for Daniel? And wasn't it wonderful that the Alperts tried so hard to keep him from missing Mama and Leah?

Daniel was safely home again, where he belonged. Everything was as it should be once more. Yet the knot in her throat and the tightness in her chest lingered and held fast, until Daniel came and put his arms around her.

"Don't worry, Leah. I still love you and Mama best in the whole world."

Mama relaxed visibly as Leah hugged Daniel. "I know," Leah told him. Swiftly as it had come, the sadness was gone; gone, too, was the unfamiliar stab of envy. "We're a family. We'll always be a family."

When it was bedtime for Daniel, Mama said, "I must run down to the drugstore. There are some things I need. I'll be back soon."

"Can Leah read to me till you come back, Mama? Please?"

Mama hesitated until Leah begged. "Please, Mama. Because I didn't get to read to Daniel at all last night."

"Just this once," Mama warned. "And make sure you keep the door locked until I come home. Don't open it for anyone."

"First read me your poem," Daniel ordered when Mama left. Leah glowed. He'd rather hear her poem than a story!

Leah didn't have to read it; she knew every word she had written.

I can dance like an elf
On the petals of a rose.
Or laugh all by myself
When I wear my laughing clothes.

I can borrow the wings
Of a passing butterfly,
Or put a dragon to sleep
With a dragon lullaby.

For when you have imagination
There is no barrier, no wall.
Oh, with imagination
I can do anything at all.

"I have imagination," said Daniel. "You want to hear what I can imagine?"

Before Leah could answer, a knock sounded on the door. Leah approached it warily.

"Who is it? Who's there?"

"Your neighbor. Gideon Brown."

Leah sighed with relief. No stranger stood waiting. Still, she was uncertain. Why had the blind man come? She hesitated, her hand on the knob. Mama had given strict orders, but she hadn't mentioned Gideon Brown.

Daniel was ready for anything that postponed bedtime. "Let him in, Leah. Maybe he'll sing for us."

So Leah swung open the door.

"Leah?" Mr. Brown asked uncertainly. "Would you ask your mother if I can come in? I have a letter I'd like her to read for me."

"Mama isn't home," Daniel called from the cot. "But Leah can read the letter. Leah is a wonderful reader."

"Can't you ask the Safers to read it?" Leah asked.

Why would he come here, when his uncle and aunt were right downstairs? Leah was ready to shut the door when he replied, "They're not home. This is their night at the movies."

Leah nodded, recalling that this was dish night. Once a week, a different dish was given free to each woman who came to the movie house. Mrs. Safer never missed going, even when she wasn't feeling too well. She had almost a complete set now.

"My letter can wait," the blind man said.

Leah, hearing the disappointment in his voice, took his arm. "That's okay. Come in. I'll read it for you."

She left the door wide open, then guided him to the

wicker chair. With a kitchen knife, she carefully slit open the envelope. A large folded sheet fell out, and drifted to the floor. Daniel leaped from the cot to pick it up.

"Hey, look. It's funny," he said. "It's got little bumps all over it."

Gideon Brown laughed. "Braille," he explained. "A special kind of writing for people like me. Let me show you."

Daniel placed the paper in Mr. Brown's hands. His eyes widened as the blind man ran his fingers over the sheet.

"A friend sent me the music I asked for," he exclaimed. "What does the letter say?"

Leah read, " 'Dear Gideon. It wasn't easy but I finally found the folk song you wanted. I look forward to hearing you sing it one of these days. George.' "

Leah stared doubtfully at the sheet of Braille. "Is that really music?"

The blind man nodded. "Listen."

As he touched the raised dots, he began to hum.

Leah was entranced. If one could hum a poem, would this be how it would sound? She spoke the words aloud without thinking.

"You've written a poem?" the blind man asked.

"Tell it to him, Leah," Daniel commanded.

Shyly, in a soft voice, Leah recited. When he made no immediate comment, she said, "You didn't like it."

"But I did. Very much. You are a child of fancies woven."

Of fancies woven. The words echoed in Leah's mind. The blind man sang music, and hummed it, and now he had spoken it.

"There's more to my poem, except I haven't written it yet," Leah said.

"Then you must finish it, of course."

"I can't always, even though I want to. Sometimes the words come hard," Leah explained.

"I know. Music sometimes comes hard, too." He seemed reluctant to leave. "I should go now."

Maybe he didn't feel like going back, to sit alone in the dark. Even as this thought passed through Leah's mind, Gideon Brown said, "This must be a lovely room. A welcoming room. I can feel it."

"It's all yellow and white," Daniel said. "Do you like yellow?"

"I don't know, Daniel. I've never seen it. Maybe Leah can describe it for me."

He and Daniel waited expectantly, while Leah pondered how to put color into words.

"I think yellow is the way the sun feels on your face on a cold winter day."

"Now white." This was a new game for Daniel, almost better than storytime.

Leah pinched her lips, thinking hard. White wasn't easy. Then she had an idea. She picked up Daniel's small pillow, filled with goose down, and brought it to the blind man.

"Feel this. It's so soft and fluffy, the way clouds look in the sky on a summer day."

"Beautiful," Gideon Brown murmured. "And blue?"

"Blue is the way a spring breeze smells, sweet and gentle."

"Red," Daniel said. "Tell him about red."

For a moment, Leah was stumped. Then, suddenly, she ran to the icebox, took out a small jar, picked up a spoon, and came back to Gideon Brown.

"Open your mouth."

Smiling, he obeyed. The smile changed to a sputter. "What in the world . . . ?"

"Horseradish," Leah said, grinning. "See? Red is fire on the tongue."

She brought him a glass of water, which he gulped down gratefully.

"Please, no more surprises," he begged, as he handed back the glass.

Daniel sighed. "Are we out of colors?"

"There's gold . . ."

"Like a ring." Gideon Brown nodded. "Smooth and cold to the touch."

"I think gold is the color of your songs," Leah said in a low voice.

There was a moment of silence. Then the blind man said, "No one has ever paid me a higher compliment. Thank you, child."

"We didn't do black," Daniel reminded them.

"I don't like black." Leah sounded angry. "Black is darkness. It's the shadows in the hall, and being lonely, and afraid. It's not being able to see . . ." She clapped her hand to her mouth. "I'm sorry."

"But you are right. To be blind is to live in unimaginable darkness."

"But you sing," Leah said in wonder. "You sing in the dark."

"Yes. How shall I explain this to you? The darkness is only in my eyes, not here," he said as he touched his forehead, "or here." He placed his hand on his heart. "And the darkness is not in my soul. Do you understand?"

Long after Gideon Brown left, long after both Daniel and Mama were asleep, Leah thought about the blind man's words.

There had been a darkness in Mama's soul, after Papa died. But now Mama had painted sunshine back into their lives.

Maybe the blind man's songs were his sunshine.

CHAPTER 9

Because Gideon Brown asked Mama to sew two white shirts for him, Mama went to a concert. And because Mama went to a concert, Mr. and Mrs. Safer came upstairs to stay with Leah and Daniel — and became family.

And this is how it happened.

Gideon Brown had come upstairs to seek Mama's help. "I have another job," he told her with much joy. "I am to sing in a fine restaurant three nights a week, and play my guitar. But I must wear a formal shirt. White, with pearl buttons. And I must also wear a black bow tie."

"It's no problem," Mama said at once. "But you will have to buy the material."

He agreed at once. "Of course I will pay for the

material. And anything else you need. And I insist on paying you for your time as well."

Leah saw the struggle in Mama's face. To charge a neighbor who was now also a friend was not right. But not to charge was to lose much needed money, for if Mama used her time to make shirts, she could not sew dresses.

Finally, Mama agreed. Gideon Brown would pay.

When the shirts were finished, and the bow tie as well, Gideon Brown invited Mama to go to a concert with him. He asked her in a slow, hesitant way, then added quickly, "If you feel you would rather not, I will understand."

Mama's eyes brightened. "I would love to go." Then her eyes lost their glow. She shook her head. "But of course I can't. I can't leave the children alone for so long a time."

Leah protested at once. "Mama, I'm ten years old. I can take care of Daniel."

Again Mama shook her head. "No. I would come home late. It is a whole evening out."

Leah heard the longing in Mama's voice.

"Maybe Mrs. Safer could stay with us, just this once, Mama. Daniel would like that, wouldn't you, Daniel?"

"Sure," Daniel agreed. He was always ready for a new experience.

Between them, Gideon Brown and Leah persuaded Mama to ask.

And so Mama went to the concert, and Mr. and Mrs. Safer came upstairs. Mr. Safer brought a checkerboard and checkers, which he placed on the table.

"I don't know that game," Daniel said, when Mr. Safer called him to the table.

"What's to know? A smart little person like you can learn in five seconds. Come. I'll show you."

Daniel was delighted. "Okay, Mr. Safer."

The old man held up his hand. "No more 'Mr. Safer'. To a checkers player like you, I am now Grandpa, understand? And to you, too, Leah. And Mrs. Safer is now Grandma."

He pointed to his wife, sitting on the sofa next to Leah, showing her how to embroider cross-stitches on a pattern held tight between two wooden hoops.

"Your Mama never showed you how to embroider?" Mrs. Safer had asked Leah.

"She never had time. She was always working."

Leah didn't mention it to Mrs. Safer, but there had been times when Papa and Mama had quarreled because when Mama couldn't get sewing jobs, she found work as a cleaning woman. Papa had been furious.

"No wife of mine goes to clean somebody else's house," he shouted.

"We can't eat pride," Mama said coldly. "Shall we let the children go hungry? Shall we wait to be thrown out because we can't pay the rent? I'll do whatever I can, and there will be no shame in it."

"A man should be able to take care of his family." Papa sank down in his chair and buried his face in his hands.

Mama went and kneeled beside him, stroking his hair. "When times are better, I won't have to work. You'll see."

But times didn't get better. After Papa died, times were worse. And now, even though Mama worked steadily, there was never money to spare.

Leah shook her head. It hurt to remember. She concentrated on the needlework.

Meanwhile, Daniel was considering Mr. Safer's suggestion seriously, his brown eyes wide and thoughtful.

"But you're not really my grandpa."

"So? Is there a law I can't be? We have no grandchildren. You have no grandparents. What a waste! So I think we should make a deal, okay? You shake my hand, and just like that" — Mr. Safer snapped his fingers — "we're in business."

Leah watched to see what Daniel would do. He gazed at Mr. Safer a moment more, then thrust his hand out. Mr. Safer shook it gravely. Then, clearing his throat, he added, "As a new grandfather, I'm entitled to at least one hug."

When Daniel threw his arms around Mr. Safer, he winked at Leah and his wife.

Whereupon Mrs. Safer leaned over and kissed Leah. "We don't shake hands. When I get a grandchild, I kiss her."

Thus the evening progressed. To no one's surprise, Daniel won every game. Leah stabbed her finger many times but persisted. Her cross-stitches were wobbly, but even so, a pattern began to appear on the cloth.

When Mama came home, Daniel was asleep on the cot, Mrs. Safer snored on the sofa, Mr. Safer dozed in the wicker chair, and Leah lay curled up like a kitten in the center of the big double bed.

It was the first of more evenings to come. And soon a once-a-week tea party was held on Monday evenings, when Gideon Brown did not have to work.

Leah was content, and even grew somewhat accustomed to having Mrs. Alpert come and pick up Daniel for an occasional overnight visit when Mama was especially busy.

Then, without warning, the contentment was shattered.

When Leah came home from school one day, Mrs. Alpert had just brought Daniel home. Daniel had immediately run downstairs to visit with the Safers. As Leah walked into the room, Mrs. Alpert was saying to Mama, "You must think of the boy's future. That must be your only concern. Think about what I've been telling you. We don't expect an answer right away."

Mrs. Alpert nodded absently to Leah. As she left, Mrs. Alpert added, "Remember. The boy's whole future is at stake."

Mama stood stricken, staring after Mrs. Alpert, her hands clasped, white-knuckled, against her chest.

Leah was alarmed. "Mama. What's wrong? What does she want?"

"Nothing. It's all right." She waved Leah away. "I can't talk now. I must think."

What could Mrs. Alpert have said that made Mama

stumble through the rest of the day with open eyes that didn't see, with sudden pauses in the midst of some task, with a need to stroke Daniel each time she passed him? This was most worrisome of all, for Mama was not a touching woman.

At bedtime, Mama allowed an extra story without being asked. When Daniel was ready to go to sleep, Mama swept him up in her arms and hugged him fiercely.

That night, in the darkness of the bedroom, the only light thrown dimly by the lampposts outside, Mama finally spoke to Leah about her problem. Mama sat as usual in the rocker; Leah leaned back against the headboard of the bed.

"Mrs. Alpert and her husband want to adopt Daniel."

Leah shot up. "Adopt Daniel? Take Daniel *away?* But he's my *brother!*"

"Shhh," Mama cautioned. "You'll wake him. The Alperts have so much to offer Daniel. Every comfort. He'll never want for anything, Leah. They will provide him with a fine education, send him to the best schools, to college. Everything I can't do, they can."

"They can't give him love, not like us," Leah said in anger.

Mama sighed. "Even that, Leah," she said, in despair. "They can give him even that. They have love to spend."

"They'll have to find some other boy. We're a family, Mama. We belong together."

But Mama wasn't listening. She ran her hands up and down her arms, as if she were chilled. Then she moaned, "I don't know what to do. I just don't know what to do."

Mama's cry of anguish pierced Leah's heart. She leaped from the bed.

"Oh, Mama," she said, clasping Mama's head to her chest.

Mama allowed the embrace for a moment. Then she said, "We must try to get some sleep now. Nothing can be decided tonight."

Leah climbed back into bed. In spite of herself, her lids grew heavy. The last thing she saw, before sleep claimed her, was Mama, swaying back and forth in the rocker, the tears she had held back all day finally coursing down her cheeks.

CHAPTER 10

Two weeks later, when Leah came home from school, Daniel was gone. He was not downstairs visiting the Safers; not playing in the hall; just gone.

Mama stood at the table, pinning a pattern to material, her face white and drawn. Leah stared at the whitc candlewick spread, untouched on the cot. She listened to the silence that filled every corner of the room. And she knew Mama had made her decision.

"You gave him away!"

Mama held up her hand, a warning gesture. She would not discuss this.

"Are you going to give me away, too, someday, if somebody asks you?"

Mama was furious. "Don't ever speak to me like

that again. This is not something a child can understand. When you are grown, and have a child of your own, then maybe you will realize —"

Leah interrupted to shout, "And what is Daniel going to think, while he is growing up? That his own mother didn't love him enough to keep him? He'll never forgive you, Mama. And neither will I. Never."

Leah ran from the room, to seek refuge in Mama's rocker. It seemed to help Mama when she was troubled. So Leah sat and stared blankly out the window, just as Mama sometimes did.

Mama did not follow. When Leah came out for the evening meal, she and Mama ate in silence. Leah moved her food around on her dish but had difficulty swallowing it. Mama seemed too withdrawn to notice.

That night Leah refused to sleep in the big double bed. Instead, she stretched out on Daniel's cot. Mama looked at her for a long moment, then went into the other room.

For the next three days, Leah spoke to Mama only when she couldn't avoid it. Again, she retreated to Mama's rocker. Brooding, she came at last to a decision.

"I'm going downstairs for a while," Leah said, speaking in Mama's general direction without looking at her.

Mama nodded. She seemed not to care about anything anymore. She probably thinks I'm going downstairs to the Safers, Leah thought. But Leah went no farther than the second floor.

She was used to the dim green lights and the shadows now. Just the same, she walked rapidly to knock on Gideon Brown's door.

He had been humming, this man who sang in the dark, but he stopped to call out, "Come in. The door isn't locked."

Leah opened it hesitantly. She knew he had no need for light, but the complete blackness of the room frightened her.

"Leah? The light probably isn't on. Just pull the cord."

Leah inched her way in, found the dangling cord, and yanked it. The overhead bulb threw just enough light that Leah could study the room.

She was surprised to see how few pieces of furniture he had. There was a narrow bed against one wall, a dresser, one easy chair, and a small table and one kitchen chair under the window.

Gideon Brown sat at the table, sheets of music in Braille spread out, his fingers tracing the markings on the paper.

"I'm learning a new song, Leah," he said.

"How did you know it was me? I didn't say anything."

"I recognized your footsteps," Gideon Brown explained.

Leah stood silent, uncertain. Upstairs, it had seemed a good idea to come, but now she was no longer sure.

"It's Daniel, isn't it?" he asked.

"Something is happening to Mama," Leah blurted, "and I don't know what to do." She began to weep. "And I know Daniel must be scared and wondering why Mama sent him away."

"The Alperts are kind and good people. They will take good care of Daniel," he said.

This was not what Leah had come to hear. She turned on him in anger. "It isn't enough. How can they be good and kind and break up our family? Do you know what Grandma Safer told me yesterday? The Alperts are going to move! To *California!* They think Daniel will forget us because he's only four years old. Then he'll really belong to them. We'll never see him again!"

Gideon's voice was gentle, but puzzled. "Why have you come to me, Leah?"

"You're our friend, aren't you? I want you to *do* something. Mama knows the Alperts are leaving. She's getting sick. She cries herself to sleep every night.

And I have nobody to read to. Nobody can read to Daniel like I can. Nobody."

"I understand, child. And I'm sorry. But what can *I* do?"

"I wish my father were here. He'd never let anybody take Daniel away."

"Leah, it was very hard for your mother to do this. She must have stayed up night after night twisting and turning in her mind what was best for Daniel."

"How can she really know what's best for him now, while he's still only four years old? How come the Safers told me they don't think it's the right thing to do? You don't think so, either, do you?"

She didn't wait for a reply, but rushed on.

"If I wasn't afraid, I'd go and get Daniel and bring him home."

"Afraid? Afraid of what?"

"Mrs. Alpert could throw me out of her house. She might not let Daniel talk to me. And even if she said I could have Daniel, Mama would be awfully mad at me. She'd probably take him right back. But I won't let her! I won't!"

"Child," Gideon Brown said in a quiet voice. "Come here. Take my hand."

She moved closer to him, then placed her hand in his.

"You trust me now, don't you, Leah? Do you remember the first time we met, on the steps?"

"I was scared of everything. The spooky lights, and all the shadows, and . . ."

". . . and especially of me." He finished the sentence. "But now you feel easier about coming and going. And though you are still somewhat uncomfortable with me, because of these sightless eyes, you and I talk to each other often. Do you know why?"

She shook her head, remembered, and said, "No."

"Because you have learned to have courage. Do you know what courage is? It's fear with a brave face."

"Do you think I have enough courage to go and get Daniel? Will you come with me? Maybe she'll have to listen if there's a grown-up there with me," Leah explained.

"All right. I'll go along. But you must understand, Leah, that we might fail to get Daniel. Don't forget your mother agreed to give Daniel to the Alperts. What makes you think Mrs. Alpert will give him up?"

"I'll beg her. I'll tell her what's happening to Mama." She drew a deep breath. Her mind was made up. "I won't go to school tomorrow. I'll just pretend that I'm going. But I'll come here."

"Then I'll expect you tomorrow morning."

Now that she had made the decision, Leah felt much

better. She looked at Gideon Brown, and watched as he ran his fingers lightly over the sheet music again. He began to hum. The sound of his humming accompanied her along the hall and up the steps.

The man who sang in the dark had courage. The thought gave her courage, too.

It was a good word. She hadn't known that fear could wear a brave face. It would have to be the face she showed to Mrs. Alpert tomorrow morning.

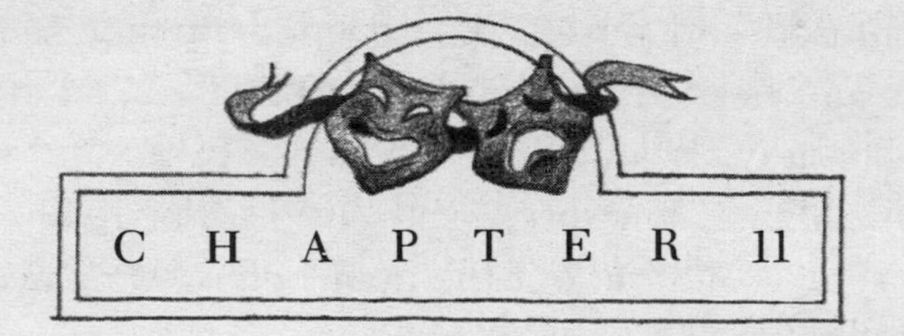

CHAPTER 11

Leah woke early but forced herself to stay in bed until she heard Mama in the kitchen. Then she washed and dressed quickly. When she came to the table, however, she left her breakfast untouched. How could she eat when she was betraying Mama, even though Mama didn't know it. Yet she was determined to carry out her plan.

"Are you sick?" Mama put her hand on Leah's forehead. "Your face is so flushed. But you don't seem to have a fever. Are you well enough to go to school?"

Leah's answer was short, almost rude. "I'm okay."

She wasn't going to school. That was lying. She'd never lied to Mama before, never on purpose, anyway. Still none of this would be happening if only Mama . . . it was all Mama's fault.

Confused and upset, she scooped up her schoolbooks and headed for the door. Mama looked at her then so sadly. Leah couldn't bear it.

"Oh, Mama. I'm sorry," she cried. "I'm really and truly sorry," and ran out the door before Mama could say a word.

As arranged, Leah stopped off at Gideon's apartment on the second floor, her schoolbooks clenched in her arms. She peered through his window till she saw Mama leave.

"We can go now," she announced. "I have the address. I got it from Mama's address book. And I know how to get there. I know which trolleys to take, and how to walk from that last trolley stop to Mrs. Alpert's house."

"I am ready whenever you say," Gideon Brown told her.

Leah guided him across the street, though he was capable of doing so by himself. He was her friend, and she was his friend now as well. When he touched her elbow, she did not wince away. She helped him up the trolley step like a mother bird with an injured chick, and seated him near the front of the car.

Once they were under way, Leah was silent. Worry had grown razor-sharp talons that clawed at her stom-

OCERY
RENT

ach. She closed her mind to the lurching of the trolley, to the stops and starts, to the clanging bell, and concentrated on not disgracing herself by throwing up.

The blind man seemed to understand. He, too, remained silent, but his hand stole out to clasp hers, and its strength and warmth began to renew her courage.

When they left the second trolley, she was concerned about the long walk, but Gideon Brown sniffed the air, held his head up to the breeze, and said it was a perfect day for a homecoming for Daniel.

"It must be quite beautiful here," he added.

Leah looked around carefully. She stopped short, grasping Gideon Brown's arm. "It is beautiful. Do you think I'm wrong? To take Daniel away, when he can live in a real house, and have trees and flowers all around . . ." Her voice trailed off.

"If you've changed your mind, we can turn around and go back," he told her. "It's not too late."

Leah thought for a moment. Then she shook her head. "No. We've already lost Papa. We're not going to lose Daniel, too."

The blind man reached out to take her hand. Leah could feel new courage steadying her at his touch.

Hand in hand, silently, they continued to walk the length of the street.

At the house, Leah turned to ask, "Will you come in with me?"

"No, Leah, I have no right to interfere."

"Not to talk. You don't have to say a word," she pleaded. "Just be there. Maybe Mrs. Alpert will know I'm serious if there's another grown-up in the room."

He yielded, but Leah could tell he was reluctant.

Before they started up the walk, Leah thought she noticed a curtain move in a window on the second floor of the house. Was Daniel at the window? She decided it was only the glitter of sun on the glass pane.

She rang the bell, touched her face to feel if it was brave, and waited.

It was only a moment, though it felt longer, before the door swung open.

"Leah!" Mrs. Alpert was surprised. "Is something wrong? Did your mother send you?"

"No. This was my idea. Can we come in?"

"Of course." Mrs. Alpert stepped to one side. As soon as they entered the foyer, Mrs. Alpert turned to Gideon Brown.

"You're the man who lives in the same building. I've heard a great deal about you. And about Mr. and Mrs. Safer, too. But I don't understand, Mr. Brown. Why are you here?"

"Don't talk to him. Talk to me," Leah said. "I've come to get Daniel." She tried to keep her voice steady, and was angry with herself because it quavered.

Mrs. Alpert was puzzled. "What do you mean . . .?"

Leah interrupted. "I mean I came to get Daniel. I'm taking him home."

Mrs. Alpert put her hand out, as if to touch Leah's hair. Leah shied away.

Mrs. Alpert turned to Gideon Brown. "Hasn't her mother explained about the adoption? And that it takes time, which is why we wanted Daniel to come and stay with us now, so he could get used to the idea. Doesn't she know her mother agreed to all this?"

Though she spoke to Gideon Brown, Mrs. Alpert glanced at Leah to see if she understood.

"Speak to Leah," the blind man said. "This is a matter for you to settle between you."

"You had no right to take him."

"Oh, child," Mrs. Alpert said. "You don't seem to understand —"

"No. I don't. I don't understand how you could come to our house and take my brother away from us. I don't understand why Mama has to cry herself to sleep every night."

Mrs. Alpert tried to interrupt, but Leah raced on.

"I don't understand why you have to come and make a big hole in our lives. All you care about is how you feel, what you want. There are lots of kids who don't have fathers or mothers, who don't even have a home. Why don't you adopt somebody who really needs you? Why does it have to be Daniel? He's *ours*."

Mrs. Alpert explained, "I only want what is best for your brother. We can do so much for him. We must think of him."

"No," Leah shouted. "That's what you told Mama. Maybe that's even what you told yourself. But all you really want is a child, a son. You stole Daniel from us, because you fell in love with him. And you broke Mama's heart."

Mrs. Alpert turned helplessly to Gideon Brown. "Please," she pleaded. "Say something. Tell her that's not the way it is."

"You tell her," the blind man said, softly. "Can you convince her? Can you convince yourself?"

At that moment, a voice cried from the stairway, "Leah! I knew you would come. I waited and waited for you."

Daniel raced down the steps, in his arms the large clown doll Mrs. Alpert had given him. He went directly to Mrs. Alpert. "Here." He thrust the clown doll at her. "I don't need this anymore. I'm going home now."

Mrs. Alpert kneeled down to embrace him. "Oh, Daniel. Don't you like it here?"

"Sure," he agreed, cheerfully. "But it doesn't have Mama and Leah. So now I want to go home."

The joy in his face as he turned to his sister and her fierce hug as she enclosed him in her arms made Mrs. Alpert step back, as if a circle had been drawn that closed her out. She waited a moment, then said in a husky voice, "Won't you say good-bye to me, Daniel?"

"Sure."

He gave Mrs. Alpert a smacking kiss on the cheek. Then he turned and clutched Leah's hand. "Okay. Let's go. Come on."

When Gideon Brown and Daniel and Leah reached the sidewalk, Leah looked back. Mrs. Alpert was standing in the doorway, twisting a handkerchief in her fingers.

"Wait a minute," Leah said. "There's something I have to do."

She ran back. "I'm sorry," she said to the tearful woman. "I'm really and truly sorry."

Mrs. Alpert whispered, "Yes, I know," and went into the house.

* * *

On the way home, Leah wondered why she didn't feel excited and happy. She had accomplished what she had set out to do. But she couldn't forget Mrs. Alpert's face.

At home, however, she pushed it out of mind when Mama, at the sight of Daniel, stood frozen. Then, her eyes radiant, her face joyful, she scooped him up and held him as if she would never let him go again.

That night, in bed, Leah stared at the ceiling and thought about two masks she had seen in one of her storybooks. One showed laughter, the other sorrow. Why did it have to be so?

Mrs. Alpert's laughter; Mama's sorrow.

Mama's joy; Mrs. Alpert's pain.

CHAPTER 12

Where had the time flown? It seemed to Leah only yesterday that Mrs. Alpert had stolen Daniel away. For weeks after that day, a feeling of dread had swept over her as she lay in bed, trying to fall asleep. Her mouth dry, heart sinking, she would tiptoe into the other room to make certain Daniel was still there.

Then came a letter from Mrs. Alpert. They had moved to California; and they had made plans to adopt a three-month-old baby boy. Mrs. Alpert's happiness shone through every word.

Leah seized Daniel and whirled him round and round the room.

"That's so wonderful. That's so marvelous," she shouted.

Rescuing Daniel had been right; she'd never

doubted that. Still a sense of guilt had lingered. She had hurt Mrs. Alpert, torn Daniel from her as Mrs. Alpert had torn Daniel from Mama and Leah. But now, at last, she could be free of that guilt. There were happy endings after all, just as in fairy tales.

When she and Daniel and Mama walked into the Safer's kitchen for their Monday evening tea, she was bursting with the good news.

"So," Mrs. Safer said. "She'll have a child of her own after all. I'm glad for her. Very glad."

"As we all are," Gideon Brown added. On impulse, Leah ran to him and kissed his cheek.

"Thank you, Leah." His voice was pleased. "What did I do to deserve that?"

"It's because you helped me when I needed you and everything turned out all right."

"How come everybody is kissing him?" Daniel wondered.

Mr. Safer looked all around. "Everybody? Who is this everybody?"

"Mama was kissing him. They were holding hands and kissing. I saw them. In the hall."

"No you *didn't!*" Leah flared. "That's a lie."

"Daniel doesn't lie," Mr. Safer said. "Anyway, why are you so excited? It's about time. Two lonely people who like each other, have respect for each other, understand one another. Why shouldn't they kiss and hold hands. Listen, young lady," he told Leah, frowning at her. "In your fairy tales, don't people fall in love and get married? Love makes the world go round. Don't you know that?"

"Leah," Gideon explained, "it was because I had just told your mother my wonderful news."

Leah sat back in her chair and relaxed. She could understand now. Good news did make you feel like hugging or kissing someone.

"Are you all ready for this?" Gideon Brown went on. The happiness in his face seemed to light up his sightless blue eyes. "I'm going to have a radio program. My *own* program. I'm going to sing and play my guitar for fifteen minutes from Mondays to Fridays at five o'clock."

Mama said, beaming at everyone, "And it's going to be called *The Wandering Minstrel.*"

Mrs. Safer reached across the table and patted Gideon's hand. "And from this you are sure to make a fine living."

"A very fine living," he agreed.

"And Gideon is giving us a radio as a gift, so we can listen to him," Mama told them.

"Can we listen to other programs, too?" Daniel

wanted to know. "I listened to lots of programs at the Alperts'."

The grown-ups laughed.

"Be my guest," Gideon Brown said.

How could so many wonderful things happen all at once? Leah marveled. There seemed to be no end to the good news tonight.

And then Mr. Safer cleared his throat. "This is maybe not the right time —" he stopped, and looked at his wife, who motioned him to go on. He began again. "There is never a right time, and Mrs. Safer and I can't wait any longer. We have something to tell you."

Mrs. Safer interrupted. "For a long time now, standing in the store has been harder and harder —"

"We didn't know what to do," Mr. Safer broke in. "We didn't know how much longer we could work. But without the store, what would we live on? And then one day a man walked in and said he was interested in buying us out. Just like that, out of the clear blue sky. He wants the store, the building — everything!"

Mama's forehead creased with worry lines. "But if you sell, what about us? Will the new owner let us stay?"

The Safers shook their heads.

"That's why it was so hard to tell you," Mr. Safer said. "He has big plans. He's going to remodel the building. Make offices on the second and third floors. Rent to professional people — doctors, dentists, whatever."

"Professional people can pay more rent." Mrs. Safer sounded apologetic. She turned to Mama. "We're old. How long could we keep up the store? So we're signing the papers tomorrow. We don't have to get out right away. He's giving us all a month."

"What will we do?" Leah cried out in panic. "Where will we go?"

Mr. Safer said sadly, "What can I tell you, child? Leave it to your Mama. She is a strong woman."

"Never mind us," Mama said. "What will you do?"

"We're not sure. Maybe we'll buy a little house. Before we couldn't afford it; now with the money from this sale . . ."

"I always wanted to live in a regular house," Mrs. Safer said with a wistful sigh. "It may not be for long, but even when you're seventy, it's nice to have a dream come true."

"We've already started looking," Mr. Safer admitted.

The tea party was over.

There was no singing that evening.

CHAPTER 13

Somehow it seemed natural for Gideon Brown to come back to their apartment with Leah, Daniel, and Mama. Since he started taking Mama out, Gideon Brown knew his way around the apartment. He went directly to the wicker armchair.

Mama sank down on the sofa, with her hands clasped tightly in her lap.

Leah and Daniel sat on the cot, waiting expectantly.

"Daniel, you should be getting ready for bed."

Leah could tell Mama said this automatically. Usually Daniel was very good about bedtime, but tonight he rebelled.

"You're going to talk. I can tell. And I want to hear. I'm part of this family," he said.

"There's nothing to talk about, Daniel," Mama began, but Gideon Brown interrupted her.

"I think we have lots of things to discuss, and I think Leah and Daniel should hear what we have to say, for it will affect them, too."

Mama shook her head. When she spoke, it made Leah think Mama was almost talking to herself.

"And so it begins all over again." Mama's voice sounded dreary. "Looking for an apartment. Being turned away because I'm a widow with young children. I thought I was through with all that . . ."

Leah couldn't bear Mama's hopelessness. She put in quickly, "You haven't even let Gideon say anything."

"I will have to look for another place, too," Gideon began. "And landlords aren't quick to rent to a blind man. We have a common problem in a way. But I've been thinking . . . it's not a new idea for me, and I haven't had the courage to mention it before, but I think I should tell you now."

"What? What?" Daniel asked with great impatience.

"Everybody's talking but nobody is saying anything," Leah added.

"If we were to marry . . . wait, let me finish," he said, though no one had spoken. "With a working husband, you wouldn't be turned away. We could even buy a house, with my earnings, and if you continue to work."

"How would that help you?" Leah asked.

"I would have a family to come home to." He turned his face toward the sofa, toward Mama. "I have come to love you all. In a way, loving you has often made it worse for me, for it has made me feel even lonelier . . . there is so much love here, I thought there might be enough for me, too."

He fell silent.

Was that why the blind man sang in the dark? Leah wondered. To push back the loneliness?

When Mama said nothing, Gideon started to rise. "I understand. It was too much, to expect that you would even consider . . ."

"Oh, Gideon," Mama said.

How sad, Leah thought, that he couldn't see the love in Mama's eyes. But maybe that wasn't important, for Mama went to his side and clasped his hand. "Neither one of us has to be lonely again," she whispered.

Daniel asked, "Is this more good news? Are you going to kiss again?"

Mama and Gideon smiled at him. To answer his question, Gideon lifted Mama's hand to his lips.

"Will we have to call you Papa?" Leah asked. "Because I won't."

Gideon Brown's response was quick. "No, Leah. Of course not. I hope to be a good father to you and Daniel, but I want you to go on calling me Gideon. I

know your Papa will always have a special place in your heart."

"You will be Leah Berk Brown. And Daniel will be Daniel Berk Brown. So Papa will still live for us, and his name be remembered," Mama added.

"Okay," Daniel said.

"Leah?" Gideon Brown asked.

Mama married? To a blind man? No, Leah told herself, not to a blind man. To Gideon, who was kind and understanding, who had given her courage, a man who could sing in the dark.

"Will we really live in a house?" Daniel asked. "Like the Alperts?"

"Not like the Alperts. And not in West Philadelphia," Mama told him. "But a house of our own . . ."

"Mama!" What Mama said triggered a thought in Leah's mind. Wasn't that what Mrs. Safer wanted, the dream she had? "Why couldn't Grandpa and Grandma Safer live with us? Then we'd be a whole family, like other people, with a grandfather and a grandmother."

"We don't even know if they would want to," Mama said.

"You could ask. You could go downstairs and ask them right now," Daniel ordered. "And Leah could read to me until you come back. You don't have to hurry," he added. "I don't mind staying up."

But the visit downstairs took longer than Daniel imagined, for when they returned, he was sound asleep, and Leah lay curled up on the sofa, in some dreamland of her own.

It was funny, Leah thought, the way bad things and good things got all mixed up together. When the Safers had made their announcement, Mama looked as if the world had come to an end. One minute she'd been so happy; the next minute she was miserable. Happiness seemed to come and go, sometimes disappearing in the wink of an eye. Well, maybe people aren't supposed to be happy all the time.

Daniel broke into Leah's thoughts.

"Is it almost my birthday?"

"I told you and told you. It's next week."

"I can't wait," Daniel decided. "Let's have my birthday now."

Leah shook her head. "It doesn't work that way."

"Will Mama come home soon? I don't have anything to do. Play with me, Leah."

"I have to finish my homework."

"You can talk to me, can't you? Tell me again about the house."

Leah pushed her homework aside. For the past three weeks, Mama had been looking for a house. Sometimes Mr. Safer went searching on his own, leaving his wife behind to take care of the store.

It was Mama who found the house just a few days ago. The Safers closed the store for the day; Mama took time off from her sewing; Gideon stopped working on his music. Even Leah was kept home from school. Again it was a two-trolley ride to get to the house. The neighborhood wasn't the least bit like West Philadelphia. But the house stood on a dead-end street on a fair-sized plot of ground.

Everyone stood quietly for a moment, staring at the house.

"It's so *big*," Daniel said.

Mama hugged him. "Yes, it is. Isn't it wonderful?"

She motioned them up the walk. "There are three steps up to the porch," she warned Gideon.

"A porch," Mrs. Safer sighed. "A house with a porch." She dabbed at her eyes with a handkerchief. "I don't have to see anything else. I'm satisfied."

But Mama urged them all in, opening the door with the key the real estate agent had given her.

"You trust me with the key?" Mama had asked him with surprise.

He had shrugged his shoulders. "That big barn of a house has been empty for years. The owner would give the key to anybody to take it off his hands."

The rooms were large; the ceilings high; their footsteps echoed on the wooden floors. There were rooms upstairs and down, a sun parlor, and a back yard, with a real tree and a few scraggly bushes.

"And the kitchen." Mama was acting as the guide. "It's perfect for a family."

Now Mama and Gideon and the Safers had to arrange for the purchase, and it all had to be done quickly. The new owner of the building where they now lived agreed to give them extra time, but no more than a month, he had insisted.

"You'll have your own room, and so will I. And Grandpa and Grandma Safer will have a big bedroom on the ground floor, the one that faces the back yard," Leah told Daniel.

"Are you glad they're coming to live with us?" Daniel wanted to know. But he didn't wait for Leah's reply. "I'm glad. We never had a grandfather and a grandmother before. It's nice. I like it."

"I do, too, Daniel."

What else was nice, Leah thought, was that everyone was contributing to the purchase of the house and furniture. Mama had said it would take a while to furnish the rooms, but they could start on the ones

they needed most. Gideon's money, Mama's money, the Safers' money. That was how a family worked.

"We'll be a real family," Daniel said. "Just like other people."

Daniel was too young to understand, Leah thought. It was far more than that. It was as if, as separate people, some part of each of them was missing. Mama without a husband; Gideon alone and blind; Leah and Daniel needing a father; the Safers longing for grandchildren. They had all been like pieces of an unfinished puzzle; when fit together, the puzzle became a beautiful picture.

Leah went back to her homework, while Daniel wished again and again, aloud, that his birthday would hurry and come. This birthday was most important, for Daniel would be five. Now he would go to kindergarten. He'd be a schoolboy. He would be big, like Leah.

His birthday came at last. Daniel shot down the steps ahead of Mama and Leah, and opened the door to the Safers' kitchen, shouting, "We're here! We're here!"

Gideon Brown had already arrived. Mama went to sit beside him, as usual. Mrs. Safer placed the customary items on the table — the lump sugar in its glass bowl, the tall glasses for tea, and hot chocolate for Leah and Daniel.

In the center of the table was the birthday cake, with swirls of blue-tinted whipped cream flowers, and six candles.

"You made a mistake, Grandma Safer," Daniel said. He could easily count up to one hundred and often did, whether you wanted him to or not. "You put six candles on the cake."

"Of course six. Five for your birthday. And one to grow on."

"And now Gideon will sing," Daniel announced, when everyone had declared that the cake was delicious, but not another piece, thank you, and Mrs. Safer had cleared the table.

"In a minute. First I have something to say to Leah," Gideon said. "Do you remember, some time ago, when you read one of your poems to me, the one with the laughing clothes?"

"I never finished it," Leah said.

"I know. I thought you wouldn't mind if I did."

"You finished it?" Leah was delighted. "Can Mama read it to us?"

"Better than that, I think. I've set it to music. Listen. I call it 'Leah's Song.' "

The music filled the room, a sprightly melody to fit

Leah's lilting words. Then it turned plaintive, as the last verse did. And when he sang the last words

They say I am of fancies woven
And dream too many dreams.
The world prefers the doers,
Or so it often seems.
For doers make the world go round,
And that, of course, is true.
But oh, for songs and fantasies
The world needs dreamers, too.

Leah felt as if Gideon's sightless blue eyes could see her at last.

And she knew that for all of her days she would remember the making of a family, and the man in the dark who had created "Leah's Song."

About the Author

ETH CLIFFORD was born in Manhattan. She has written dozens of books for children; among them *Just Tell Me When We're Dead* and *Help! I'm a Prisoner in the Library.* Ms. Clifford now makes her home in North Lauderdale, Florida.